BLOOMERS!

by Rhoda Blumberg

illustrated by Mary Morgan

Bradbury Press · New York
Maxwell Macmillan Canada · Toronto
Maxwell Macmillan International
New York · Oxford · Singapore · Sydney

Bradbury Press
Macmillan Publishing Company
866 Third Avenue
New York, NY 10022

Maxwell Macmillan Canada, Inc.
1200 Eglinton Avenue East
Suite 200
Don Mills, Ontario M3C 3N1

Macmillan Publishing Company is part of the Maxwell Communication
Group of Companies.

First edition
Printed and bound in the United States of America
10   9   8   7   6   5   4   3   2   1
The text of this book is set in Berling.
Typography by Julie Quan
The illustrations are watercolors.

LIBRARY OF CONGRESS CATALOGING-IN-PUBLICATION DATA
Blumberg, Rhoda.
Bloomers / by Rhoda Blumberg ; illustrated by Mary Morgan — 1st ed.
p.   cm.
Summary: How that new-fashioned outfit, bloomers, helped Amelia Bloomer,
Elizabeth Cady Stanton, and Susan B. Anthony spread the word
about women's rights.
ISBN 0-02-711684-0
1. Women's rights—United States—History—Juvenile literature.
2. Trousers—United States—History—Juvenile literature.
3. Foundation garments—United States—History—Juvenile literature.
4. Costume—United States—Symbolic aspects—Juvenile literature.
I. Morgan, Mary, date.   II. Title.
HQ1236.5.U6B58   1993
305.42'0973—dc20   92-27154

For my granddaughters
Carla, Ilana, Melodica, Amalia, Dana, Eliza
–R.B.

℘

For my son, Dylan
–M.M.

A tight corset that pinched the waistline and squeezed the chest! At least four layers of petticoats — including one made with scratchy horsehair — to puff out the skirt! A heavy dress long enough to hide feet and sweep the floor! In the 1850s, respectable women who wanted to look fashionable wore these uncomfortable clothes.

When Libby Miller visited the small town of Seneca Falls, New York, in 1851, she was dressed in a costume that shocked everyone.

She wore a pair of ballooning trousers that hugged
the ankles, topped by a dress that seemed more like a
blouse because it was short — just to the knees.

In those days proper females *never* wore trousers, and *never* showed their ankles. They walked slowly, hampered by heavy clothes, and they stood as stiff as statues because corsets dug into their flesh when they slouched or bent over.

Libby had freed herself from the female's "cage" during her honeymoon in Europe. She wanted to enjoy hiking in the Swiss mountains without wearing a long dress and a tightly laced corset. Why be cramped by clothing at any time?

She purchased an outfit that had been designed for
women who hoped to gain strength at health resorts. This
free-spirited young lady decided to wear this costume
every day — with her husband's approval (of course).

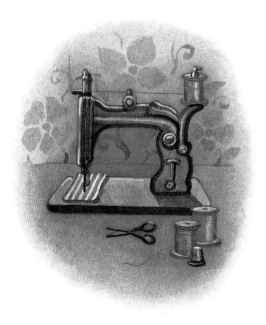

Libby had come to Seneca Falls to visit her best friend, cousin Elizabeth Stanton, another woman with a mind of her own. Many people called Elizabeth a "radical revolutionary" because she believed that women deserved all the opportunities given to men — including the right to vote.

If men could wear pants, she could, too. When she saw Libby wearing an outfit that wasn't a "clothes prison," Elizabeth immediately made black satin pants and a dress that barely reached her knees.

Her father, Judge Cady, was very upset when he heard about her costume. He wrote to her that no woman of good sense would make a "guy" of herself, and that he hoped she would not visit him wearing the outlandish outfit. Elizabeth's oldest son was also embarrassed. He begged his mother not to show up at his boarding school wearing her trousers.

Elizabeth was stubborn. Life was easier when she
wore her new "immodest" outfit.

She could climb stairs with a baby in one hand and a
candle in the other. She didn't have to worry about trip-
ping on a skirt.

It was such a relief to take long strides and to breathe freely without a confining corset that Elizabeth told her friend Amelia Bloomer about it. Amelia was editor of *The Lily*, a journal "devoted to the interests of women." Its main purpose was promoting "temperance" — by banning liquor and denouncing drunkards.

When Amelia saw Elizabeth's pants and minidress, she decided that women needed freedom not only from drunken husbands but also from cumbersome, crippling clothes.

Ladies who were slaves to fashion were foolish. They were clamped by corsets, weighed down by petticoats, and hobbled by gowns that swept dust from floors and trash from streets. Amelia Bloomer promoted the pants costume by publishing a picture of it in *The Lily.* "We shall be allowed breathing-room," she wrote, "and our forms shall be what nature made them."

Piles of letters arrived from women who wanted sewing instructions for the outfit. They were happy to pack away their corsets, petticoats, and floor-length dresses. Newspaper reporters named the new style "bloomers."

Interest in bloomers increased subscriptions to *The Lily*. Then Amelia decided to enlighten her readers about women's rights. After reading a book called *Ruling a Wife*, which praised wives who "submit to and obey" their husbands, she wrote that females were not "parlor ornaments or mere playthings for man," and that a woman is "man's equal, and not his slave." Amelia welcomed "radical" articles by Elizabeth, who insisted that women should be allowed to run for office, and that they must demand the right to vote.

There was another woman who joined the crusade for female freedom. She was Susan B. Anthony. Susan had been Amelia's houseguest in 1851 when she attended an antislavery meeting at Seneca Falls. At first Susan was shocked by the bloomers worn by Amelia and Elizabeth. However, she was not put off by their ideas. She became passionately involved in the women's rights movement. It took a while for her to give up long skirts because she feared that as an unmarried, unattractive "old maid," she would be the butt of nasty jokes if she wore a short skirt and pants. Within a year, however, she not only donned bloomers but also had her hair cut short by James at the Seneca Falls Barber Shop — to defy notions about acceptable ladylike fashion.

Determined to get their message across, Amelia, Elizabeth, and Susan traveled to towns and cities on lecture tours.

At that time properly brought-up women were expected to act frail and helpless. They *never* traveled unless they were escorted by a male. And they were not supposed to speak in public. It was bad manners.

How shocking it was to hear lady lecturers and see them wearing bloomers! Men hooted at them. Newspapers made fun of them. And quite a few women called their costume vulgar and their ideas outrageous.

Timid ladies who came to look and laugh or be horrified by bold, pants-wearing females stayed to listen and learn. Bloomers became the *reform dress* that symbolized women's demand for equal rights, including the right to vote.

Bloomers went out of fashion, but not the idea the costume represented: *WOMEN'S RIGHTS*.